MY JOURNEY

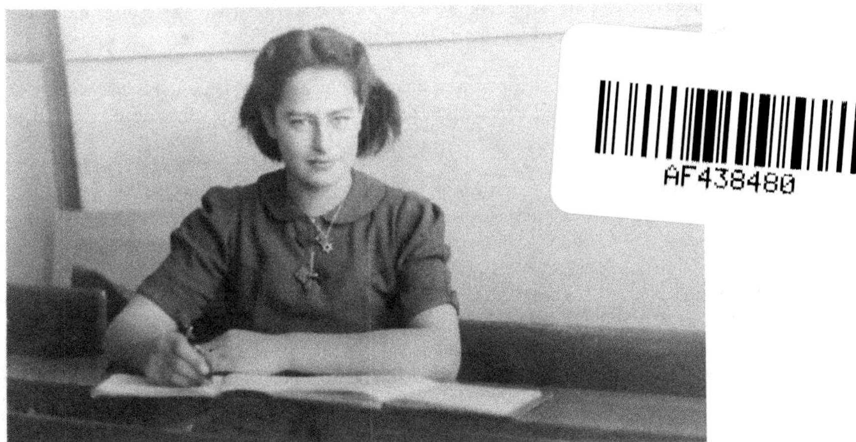

Spring, 1940

100th Birthday Celebration
November 2023

by Carla Olman Peperzak

As narrated to her daughter,
Marian Peperzak Cummings

innovativeink
PUBLISHING
A Division of Kendall Hunt

Cover images © Rose Birashk and Carla Olman Peperzak

www.innovativeinkpublishing.com
Send all inquiries to:
4050 Westmark Drive
Dubuque, IA 52004-1840

Published in the United States of America

Dedication

I am dedicating this chronicle of my experiences during World War II and the Holocaust in the Netherlands to all students and staff who pass through the doors of Carla Olman Peperzak Middle School.

I also dedicate this chronicle to my family, past, current, future, and in special memory of those who perished in Holocaust.

I was a Second Lieutenant in the Royal Dutch Army Nurse's Corps. Fall, 1946.

"nazi"

Very intentionally the word "nazi" will never
be capitalized in this memoir.

Table of Contents

Carla Peperzak Middle School opened in September 2023 in Spokane, Washington.

Andre Wicks, first Peperzak Middle School Principal and me with the future first student body.

It is a reality! I attended the School Dedication with available family members, October 2023.

Foreword

In 2004, an 80-year-old woman moved from Colorado Springs, Colorado to Spokane, Washington. She had already lived all over the world and socialized with dignitaries and political leaders. Her husband had passed away in Colorado 3 years earlier and her daughter lived in Spokane. In a very short time, it seemed that 'everyone' knew Carla Peperzak. She was not a reclusive widow! Carla quickly made connections at the retirement community where she lived. She was known by those who regularly attended the Spokane Symphony concerts. Carla also connected with the Spokane Jewish community, via the synagogue and the Spokane chapter of Hadassah, the Women's Zionist Organization of America.

My husband and I have been involved in planning the Spokane Community Observance of the Holocaust since 1995. When we learned that Carla was a Holocaust survivor, I went out to lunch with her to get to know her better and hear her story. Soon thereafter, she joined our planning committee and has continued to be a valued and involved member. Since then, our friendship has grown. My own parents were Holocaust survivors, and my mother was born only a few months before Carla. I felt a strong connection. My life has been tremendously enriched by knowing Carla. Her wisdom, resilience, calm demeanor and her personal history are an ongoing inspiration. She is a woman of valor, a true "Eshet Chayil"*.

Carla did not speak about her experiences during World War II until 1992, when her granddaughter read The Diary of Anne Frank in middle school. She had been silent for 50 years. Megan knew that her grandmother had grown up in Amsterdam and lived near the Frank family but did not realize that during the Holocaust, her grandmother Carla had worked with the Dutch underground, that she saved lives while risking her own.

After moving to Spokane, Carla gradually began to share her story. Over the years, she has spoken to innumerable students - from middle school to college classes, to religious groups, to business organizations. Her audiences are enthralled to hear the accented voice of a true hero. Carla is committed to sharing the reality of the Holocaust, to call out injustice, and to teach the lesson of respecting others. She aspires to prevent atrocities like the Holocaust from ever happening again.

I've had the privilege of assisting Carla on several occasions as she has done her presentation. Her Power Point slides are simply a trigger for her to tell some of her many, many stories. Each presentation is slightly different; it is part history lesson, part personal anecdotes, always honest and always evoking emotion. It is awesome to witness and moving to watch how students react and to see Carla's interaction with them while answering questions.

Carla has won many awards and received many well-deserved accolades, including Washingtonian of the Year in 2020, honorary doctorate degrees from Washington State University and Gonzaga University, and has had a Spokane middle school named after her. Carla insists that she doesn't feel that these awards and honors are about HER but appreciates that they are a means of sharing her story and spreading her message.

Carla celebrated her 100th birthday on November 7, 2023. She admits that she is slowing down a little bit. This book is an attempt to make Carla's story available to a broader audience and especially to students who may not have the opportunity to hear Carla in person. Carla's daughter, Marian Cummings, transcribed her mother's story. It is written in Carla's voice, as a first-person narrative, so that the reader can "hear" Carla speak.

I hope that Carla's life journey inspires you, the reader, to respect others and to remember Carla Peperzak.

Mary Noble MD, Spokane, Washington
September 2024.

*Proverbs 31, v.10-31

Carla in 1940 at the start of the war

Prologue

I was sixteen years old when World War II started. After the war ended I only wanted to go on with life and forget about the atrocities that happened to my family and friends during those years of the war. I did not want to think or talk about what I experienced as a teenager and young adult.

However, it was impossible to forget.

It took me 55 years to be able to openly talk about what I lived through. It was very, very difficult to bring up the memories and speak about those years. However, I realized how important it is to educate others on the events that took place in order for everyone to remember and prevent this history from repeating itself.

Never again.

Acknowledgements

Thank you, thank you, thank you - to all the wonderful people who spent so much time, energy, and expertise to help me get this book published.

Daughter Marian who did all the writing, editing, and so much more.

Friend Kimberly Burnham who did the editing, formatting, and initial publishing of this book. Both spent endless hours to make this book possible.

Daughters Joan and Yvonne who helped retrieve and sort many of the photos and pictures in this book and spent considerable time proofreading.

Great granddaughter Rose, age 11, who used her artistic ability to create the artwork that is displayed on the cover of "My Journey."

Great grandson Cole who helped with writing the back cover of this book and who used his talent to draw the beautiful train for "My Journey."

Friend Mary Noble for writing the foreword and all her support over the years.

Son Marc who gave me the inspiration to write a man-
uscript dedicated solely to my experiences during World
War II.

Train drawn by my great grandson Cole Birashk age 14.

Germany's Sophistication & The Holocaust

Germany started World War I, which they lost. Germany was then forced to sign a peace treaty known as the Treaty of Versailles after their surrender. The terms of the treaty were extremely harsh causing severe inflation, which made living conditions very difficult throughout the country. The German population was desperate for change, which Adolf Hitler promised if he was voted as chancellor of the republic. He was elected chancellor in 1933. Despite the poor economy between World War I and World War II Germany was still advanced in culture, medicine, education and the arts. Hitler blamed the Jews for all of Germany's financial problems.

Education was mandatory and historically very strict. Students were required to follow the rules without question, good or bad. Consequently, when Hitler came into power, the majority of German citizens accepted his orders and decrees without question. He encouraged antisemitism in particular.

If nazism could happen in an advanced civilized society such as Germany, it can happen in any country at any time. I hope and pray that this will never happen again.

Map Of Europe.

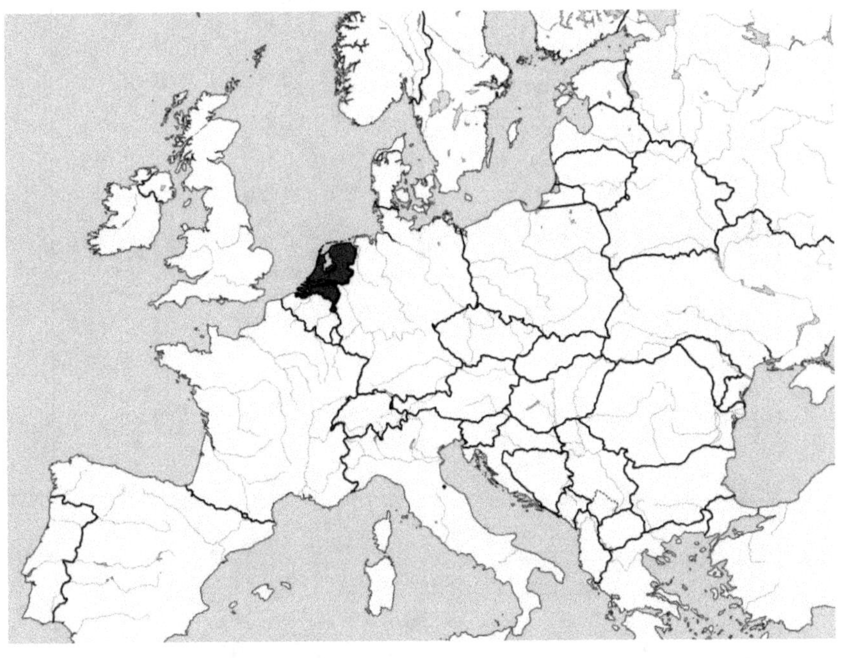

Notice how small the country of the Netherlands is in relation to the rest of Europe.

Map Of The Netherlands.

The Netherlands

The Netherlands is a small country in Western Europe. Its size is similar to the state of Maryland. 41 states in the USA are larger. In 2024, there were a little over 17 million people in the Netherlands.

When I was growing up there were 9 million people. North of the Netherlands is Scandinavia, east is Germany, south is Belgium, and to the west is the North Sea and Great Britain. North to south is approximately 300 km (190 miles), east to west is approximately 260 km (160 miles). Because we were so close to so many countries it was mandatory that we learned French, German, and English in addition to our own Dutch language in school.

Many people call The Netherlands Holland. Netherlands means "low land." The Netherlands has 12 provinces, two of which are called North Holland and South Holland. They have the largest population in the country because the big cities are there. Amsterdam is in North Holland while Den Haag and Rotterdam are in South Holland. Much of North and South Holland is below sea level. The original windmills were built to pump the water from the land. Today they no longer use windmills to pump water but rely on electric pumps.

What is interesting, in the 1930's a dam was built across the Zuider Zee, part of the North Sea. The lake that was created was named the IJsselmeer. Fifty years after the dam was built the houses in Amsterdam, which were built some three hundred years ago on very long wooden pilings driven into the original salty water, started tilting because the pilings started rotting in the resulting sweet water. The foundations of these buildings are now being repaired but it is extremely expensive.

The Concert Gebouw, a very beautiful acoustically perfect auditorium in downtown Amsterdam, also started tilting. What's amazing is that the building was repaired while concerts continued taking place.

I grew up and went to school in the neighborhood of the Concert Gebouw. My school was often invited to attend rehearsals. Music was an important part of my life and I attended many concerts there. The interior balcony walls of the auditorium were inscribed with the names of famous musical composers: when the nazis took control of the country they removed the names of all the Jewish composers.

I was born and raised in Amsterdam and my parents were born and raised in Rotterdam. Amsterdam had the largest Jewish population in the Netherlands. The public school I attended closed for Jewish High Holidays because so many of the students were Jewish.

My Parents and Family

My parents in the Fall of 1947

My parents grew up in Rotterdam. My mother was not born Jewish. At the age of 16 my mother, along with her younger brothers and sisters, were sent to an orphanage after their parents died in the Spanish Flu epidemic. The Spanish Flu hit the Netherlands particularly hard. It is estimated around 41,000 Dutch citizens died during the epidemic in the years 1918 to 1920. My mother was then taken in by a Jewish family. She became very familiar with Judaism, and eventually met and married my dad who was Jewish.

My father was quite artistic and chose a career in the fashion industry. The business he worked for transferred him to Amsterdam. He eventually started his own business named HODACO (HOllandse DAmes COnfectie, translated as "Dutch Ladies Ready-to-Wear") designing and manufacturing high end women's clothing. He lost his entire business during the war. After the war, the United States voted on an initiative called the Marshall Plan. It was a program that gave foreign financial aid to Western Europe to help boost their economies after WWII. Thanks to the Truman Doctrine and later the Marshall Plan, many banks came to my father offering loans to help him start his business over again. He then named his company Olman Dames Confectie.

I had a happy childhood. I had one sister who was a year older than I. Her name was Miep, a nickname for Wilhelmina. She liked completely different things than I did. I liked school and sports, especially water sports: swimming, skating, and rowing. When I was old enough all my transportation was done by bicycle. I went everywhere with the bike, rain or shine.

The nazi invasion of the Netherlands took place on May 10, 1940. It took five days before the country surrendered. It was my final year of high school and I was doing my final exams during the invasion. Final exams included oral exams but they were postponed for a month because of the invasion and subsequent occupation.

I am on my mother's lap with my sister standing next to us.

Me, my mother and my sister, Miep

Sporting Events

I am the third from the right.

On horseback.

Me, my mother and my sister.

I am the second from right. I often played goalie in field hockey.

Playing tennis (I am second from the left).

I loved all sports related to water.

Rowing became an important part of my life when I was a teenager. I belonged to a rowing club called Poseidon, which was not a Jewish club but 95% of the members were Jewish. I often practiced before school at 6:00 in the morning. The club and its activities all took place on the Amstel River. By the way, Amsterdam is named after the river: it was first called "Amstelredam."

I rowed in a four-person scull, the largest size our club had. We called it a "four." Rowing taught me discipline. One had to be very precise in order to be able to row in unison. I also rowed by myself in a single scull.

Race day on the Amstel.

I was rowing the third / starboard position in the photo.

The Poseidon Rowing Club was also socially important for my family. My sister met her beau Phil there. I met my boyfriend John Pais there. John and I were close until he and his family fled the Netherlands at the beginning of the war, eventually settling in the United States. After the war he married my cousin Zus Cats. Her sister Jopie Cats met her husband Jules Markus at Poseidon. John's sister Jetty met and married Doris Markus (Jules' brother). There were more inter-relationships, but I no longer remember them all.

1940

Year-end party in 1940 the Poseidon Club

Family And Friends

Family and friends posing in front of an apartment complex coincidently where Anne Frank's family lived before the war. I am third from the right, John Pais is standing to my left.

My boyfriend John Pais and me´ in the early 1940s

My Sister Miep And Her Beau Phil Keizer

Razzias

The nazis used "razzias" to round up and deport Jews to their concentration camps throughout the war. "Razzia" means unexpected raid or roundup. The first razzia took place in Amsterdam in February 1941. Four hundred Jewish boys and men were unexpectedly taken off the streets, were deported, and murdered. The Dutch population was shocked. They rebelled by striking against the invaders in Amsterdam, the strike rapidly spreading to the surrounding areas. All shops, factories, and transportation were shut down for three days. The nazis were surprised. They had wrongly assumed that the Dutch population would welcome their presence because, after all, the Netherlands was a "brother" nation and the citizens of both countries were all Anglo Saxon. The strike ended with brutal retaliation by the nazis who killed local citizens in the streets. The second razzia took place in Amsterdam in June 1941, which included a raid at the Poseidon Rowing Club. If you can call it fortunate, they raided the club on a Wednesday when most of the members were not present. Four of my close friends were taken that day and never seen again.

Beginning of the War

This photo is of my family at the beginning of the war. In the early days of the occupation life didn't change too much. As you can see we were at a restaurant enjoying a cup of coffee. But once the German soldiers sat down at the table next to us, we became very uncomfortable, which is demonstrated by my father pulling up the collar of his coat to partially hide his face in the photo.

Seated at our table from left to right are Phil Keizer (my sister's beau), my sister Miep, my cousin Jack de Groot, my mother, and my father.

Phil Keizer was Jewish and he carried a British passport, having been born in Great Britain. Consequently, when he was picked up, he was sent to a work camp in Germany and not to a concentration camp. His parents did not survive. Phil returned from the work camp after the war and eventually moved to the United States without my sister who had met someone else whom she later married.

My cousin Jack De Groot was a true hero. He became very important in the resistance movement and often helped me when I needed support for my underground activities. Jack was asked to do some very difficult things during the war and even after the war ended. The most difficult task he was given was to eliminate secret nazi collaborators. Jack was imprisoned for the eliminations he carried out after the war. The Dutch Government eventually learned how invaluable Jack's work in the resistance had been, released him, gave him a commendation and a lifelong pension.

Jack and his future wife Jetty

The Family Reunion

My extended family gathered for a reunion in Den Haag in the summer of 1941. Almost everyone was there, including my father's brothers and sisters and their spouses. We often gathered on Sundays before the war for a meal, conversation and music. We also frequently celebrated New Year's Eve together because one of my father's brothers was born on December 31st and another brother on January 1st. My father's family was very musical. My father's father, my grandfather, was a professional musician, and his youngest sister was a concert pianist. This photograph was the last time we were all together. Most of them were killed by the nazis.

The Olman Family, 1941.

Occupation

Immediately after the Netherlands surrendered to Germany the nazis installed an SS officer, Seyss-Inquart, as head of state. The queen, her family and some members of the Dutch Parliament fled to England. Once The Netherlands was occupied, the Germans slowly began to clamp down on the Jewish population. Slowly but surely, measure after measure was implemented against the Jewish people, taking away all their rights and privileges. In October 1940 all Jewish businesses had to be registered. In November 1940 all Jewish civil servants, teachers and university professors were dismissed from their jobs. By 1941 the Jews were already banned from all public transportation, cinemas, and many shops and stores.

Parades by the occupiers.

Bomb Shelter

This bomb shelter in Amsterdam was built before the war as a precautionary measure in fear of what might happen. They were all over town. The Netherlands had remained neutral during World War I and hoped to do so again during World War II. That was not meant to be.

A bomb shelter that was located in our neighborhood.

German Directional Signs

These signs were at the south end of Amsterdam about 4 or 5 blocks from my house. Before the signs were placed, the Germans entering the city would ask the local residents for directions. My sister, as well as other locals, delighted in giving the invaders the wrong directions.

When the northern part of the Netherlands was finally liberated in 1945 and the end of the war was declared, people celebrated by destroying anything and everything the nazis left behind. It was especially gratifying to see the German directional signs taken down and burned. Dutch nazi collaborators were arrested and imprisoned.

Pile of broken signs immediately after the Germans surrendered in 1945

Propaganda

One way the Germans tried to influence the local population was to take control of the press, force censorship, and hang propaganda posters all over the city. These posters were just a part of the nazi propaganda, which was very sophisticated, active and, unfortunately effective. They encouraged antisemitism, advertised for labor and military recruits, and bragged about Germany's war exploits. The local Dutch newspapers did the same, being under German control. They were deceptive and gave misinformation. The SS would offer exceptions to the rules for certain Jews making them feel safe, and then would unexpectedly nullify the exception and immediately round those people up. Many local residents scratched out the posters, threw paint on them, and tried to tear them down.

Two propaganda posters.

Jewish Quarter

There were no ghettos of any kind in Amsterdam prior to World War II. About a year into the occupation Jewish people were forced out of their homes in the countryside and brought to a cordoned off area in downtown Amsterdam. Many Jews lived in this section of town. The non-Jews who lived there were forced out of their homes in order to accommodate the displaced Jewish families. This area became the Jewish quarter and non-Jews were discouraged from entering. Barriers and barbed wire were posted at the borders.

During the day, the Jews living in the quarter were allowed to come and go. There was an evening curfew for the entire Dutch population.

Sign says, "Jewish Street" in German (top) and in Dutch (below).

Sign says, "Jewish Quarter" in German (top) and in Dutch (bottom)

Photos I took of the Jewish Quarter.

Restrictions

The Jewish people were prohibited from sitting on any of the benches in all the parks in Amsterdam, starting in 1941. Radios were confiscated from all Jews. Not only radios, but also bank accounts and cars. Jewish people couldn't go to beaches, pools, museums, restaurants, stores, and markets. Jewish youth weren't allowed in public schools or universities. Jews could no longer marry non-Jews. These were just a few of the many prohibitions.

Sign says, "For Jews Forbidden"

There were a few Jewish stores that were allowed to be open a few hours a day. Most of the time they ran out of items to sell.

Here is a photo I took of a Jewish vegetable store. The sign on the door says, "sold out today do not know when we will receive more supplies."

Registration and Identification

June 1941 Mandatory registration form for Jews

As of January 1941, all Jews were forced to be registered as Jews. Not every Jewish person chose to register. Those who took the risk of not registering and were lucky enough not to be betrayed, were counted among the few survivors.

In September of that year, the Jews, along with the entire population of the Netherlands received IDs and were mandated to carry their IDs at all times. The Jewish ID had a "J" next to their photograph on the card.

My original ID card had a "J" on it. With the help of a German attorney named Hans Calmeyer, my father managed to get me another ID card without a "J". It took about a year before I no longer was identified as a Jew. I'm sure I destroyed my first ID. This instantly gave me a lot of freedom. I no longer had to follow the restrictions that were put on the Jewish people. I could use my bicycle again, and travel by train, bus, or streetcar.

The back and front of a Jewish gentleman's ID card, from the archives of NIOD Instituut Voortrekker Oorlogs-en-Holocaust-Genocide Studies.

The Star

Front and back of my ID card in 1942

Every Jewish person had to wear a star as of May 1942. We were forced to buy our own stars and we had to buy more than one star because they had to be sewn onto our clothing. Each one cost 15 cents. That's $3.00 in today's world, 2024. There were strict instructions on how to wear the star: it had to be worn on one's left-hand side on the chest.

As stated above, in 1941 the nazis demanded that every Jewish person in the Netherlands register as a Jew. Approximately 168,000 of the around 175,000 Jews did so. This number included roughly 20,000 German Jews who had fled to the Netherlands between 1933 and 1939 after the nazis took control of Germany. There were a number of Jews who took the risk of not registering. It is believed 28,000

Jews went into hiding. 13,000 of those in hiding were betrayed and killed. 15,000 Jews in hiding survived the war along with 5,200 Jews who either did not register and were not betrayed, or returned from from the death camps after liberation. Of the 175,000 Jewish people living in the Netherlands at the start of World War II, just over 20,000 remained. A staggering eighty eight percent (88%) of the entire Dutch Jewish population was killed during the nazi occupation. The Netherlands lost the greatest percentage of their Jewish population of any country in the war.

Wearing our stars. This photo was taken before the "J" was removed from my ID card. I'm second from the left.

**JOODSCHE RAAD
VOOR AMSTERDAM**

Nw. KEIZERSGRACHT 58
AMSTERDAM-C.   AMSTERDAM, 29 April 1942

L. S.

Van a.s. Zondag af zal door iederen Jood de z.g. „Joden-ster" moeten worden gedragen.
De Joodsche Raad reikt deze kenteekenen uit.

Per persoon zijn **voorloopig** maximaal vier sterren verkrijg-baar. Eén textielpunt moet per vier sterren of gedeelten daarvan worden ingeleverd. De prijs per ster is vier cent.

De sterren zijn verkrijgbaar bij de plaatselijke vertegen-woordigers van den Joodschen Raad, respectievelijk op die plaatsen, waarheen U door onze functionarissen zult worden verwezen.

De ster moet zoodanig worden ingeknipt en ingevouwen, dat de zespuntige ster, met inbegrip van de stippellijn, zichtbaar op het kleedingstuk wordt gedragen.

De plaats, waar het kenteeken moet worden gedragen, is in de dagbladpers aangegeven.

                          Hoogachtend,
            JOODSCHE RAAD VOOR AMSTERDAM:

              A. ASSCHER   }
            Prof. Dr. D. COHEN } Voorzitters

N.B. De verkoop vindt uitsluitend plaats op vertoon van Uw persoonsbewijs voorzien van een J.

Document listing instructions for wearing the star. Every registered Jew received this by mail.

Anytime a Jewish person was outside of their home in the open, they had to visibly wear the star. This now included very young children, not just Jews over the age of 14.

The bridal couple in the photo collage were friends of mine, the Speyers. The photo shows the bride with the mandatory star attached to her wedding gown. Her new husband is hiding his star behind their wedding booklet. Shortly after their wedding, I helped them go into hiding. While the couple was in hiding Mr. Speyer (the groom) left his hiding place to go to his father who was dying. I ran into him by accident and told him what he was doing was very dangerous. The man was obviously distraught and told me "If I am caught you will be caught." Fortunately for both of us he was never captured.

Transfer Kamp Westerbork

In the fall of 1942 the razzias and the mass deportations of Jewish people increased a great deal. Jewish citizens continued to go into hiding. Sadly, many were betrayed, and some turned themselves in, finding it much too arduous to stay in hiding.

Kamp Westerbork, in northeastern Netherlands, was originally designed to be a refugee camp for German Jews who were fleeing their country and needed temporary housing. In July 1942 Westerbork became a transfer camp, used by the nazis to assemble the Dutch Jews. Many arrived at Westerbork by passenger train. From Westerbork they were transferred into cattle car trains destined for one of the concentration camps in eastern Europe. More than 100,000 Dutch Jews passed through Westerbork. Only a few thousand survived.

Jewish families were forced into passenger trains for transport to Westerbork (transfer) Kamp.

Boarding cattle cars for transport to the concentration camps.

Boarding cattle cars for transport to the concentration camps.

Camp Westerbork

Going to Camp Westerbork

A photo of Camp Westerbork

Hiding Wilma And Mieke

Because I was no longer identified as Jewish, an uncle of mine asked me if I knew of a place where he, his wife and his two daughters could go into hiding. I was fortunate to find the right person who helped me to find me a place for them to hide. It was quite an undertaking to get them there because all Jewish owned cars had been confiscated, one had to avoid using public transportation, and traveling together was much too dangerous. We moved them one by one via bicycle.

My cousins were Wilma, age 3 and Mieke, age 18 months old. Both girls were too young to safely go into hiding together, and could not stay with their parents: they were too young to be cooped up in a small attic room. So, we found places for each child where they became part of a Christian host family. We changed the name of Wilma to make it less Jewish and taught it to her. She easily accepted her new name while forgetting her real name. The family she was originally placed with could not keep her so they moved her to another family without informing me.

After the war, the parents and the younger daughter came out of hiding, were reunited, and returned to Amsterdam. The difficulty was finding Wilma because of her change in hiding place and change in name. With the help of a Canadian officer and his Jeep we went to the area where my cousin first went into hiding to look for her. Immediately after the war, whenever a military Jeep stopped, it would be surrounded by local children who were always given candy by the soldiers. We stopped in the town where my cousin originally went into hiding to ask for directions, and we were immediately surrounded by a group of children asking for candy. One little girl pointed at me and said "Carla?" Believe it or not that was my cousin: she found me! She took me to her foster parents who immediately understood and let her leave with me to be reunited with her family. My cousin told me later that she stayed in contact with her foster parents for many years because they had been so good to her.

Children greeting the liberators

Wilma and Mieke 1941 - 1942

Mieke, me and Wilma in Utrecht, Netherlands, May 2017

After helping my uncle and his family find a hiding place, I was asked by other friends to find them places to hide as well. I was not able to do this without the help of the people in the resistance. As a result I also became part of the resistance.

Altogether I eventually was able to help 40 people and support them while they were in hiding. I am very grateful that they all survived.

Dear Carla,

I received your email address via Tix (daughter of Kitty) from Cousin Jose (Horbach). This gave me the opportunity to get in touch with you. While you are waking up and eating breakfast here in our small country the day is almost over at least, in terms of daylight.

Carla, I was completely moved while reading this interview. Not because of the suggested ties with Anne Frank I understand those details are used for the readers to make it clear of what happened. But your story really hit home. Of course, because I was part of this period at the young age of 3 to 6 years. But especially because through your perseverance you found me in Schagen with my last hiding place parents. Know that I myself am completely convinced that I would never have developed if it hadn't been for you. I am ashamed that I never talked to you about this. I hope it is not too late to do so now.

The family Jaspers (my foster parents during the war) just gave me to you. She trusted you immediately and you brought me back to your parents' house where my mother was staying at the time. Imagine a child who was "lost" and had another name had to be found. And you did that. That afternoon I will never forget. I still remember it clearly. Happily to this day, I have been able to maintain contact with them (the Jaspers) and their children.

Not so long ago I heard about Loutje's ups and downs. Now after the interview I understood your role in it. Oh, how brave you were in those days and aware of the path you chose. And what you wrote about your mother, my Aunt Jo, I never knew either. I do know the child of the sister of your mother, Jan Arie de Groot, was also deeply involved in resistance work. He then called himself Jack (Miep gave him that name). He lived in Spain for a long time and is still alive. When he was in Amsterdam a few years ago I visited with him. On the advice from friends, I took him homemade butter cake in a tin your father always gave to his staff at Sinterklaas time. It was an emotional afternoon and very good.

Dear Carla, how good it is that you tell your story. If anyone thinks putting an end to the past and you don't talk about it, that's me. Because of that I am so happy you are doing this. Let's hope this courageous step will not be too difficult for you; and your children and grandchildren will be supportive. And that it gives you a sense of satisfaction of having talked about this once. Thank you again and who knows it would be a pleasure to stay in contact every. I would love that.

Love,
Wilma

Translation of Wilma's letter

In 2017 we had a small Olman family reunion in Utrecht, the Netherlands. My two cousins Wilma and Mieke joined us. It was good to spend some time with both of them remembering our war experiences. Wilma reminded me that I had not only rescued her once but twice, first finding her a hiding place in a small village and then finding her and returning her to her family after the war. She is grateful to this day.

Lieve Carla,

Jouw e mail adres kreeg ik via Tix (dochter van Kitty) van nicht José. Wat voor mij de
mogelijkheid was een lijntje te leggen.
Terwijl jij nu rustig wakker wordt en gaat ontbijten zit hier in ons kleine landje de dag er
alweer bijna op in ieder geval qua daglicht.

Carla, ik was helemaal ontroerd tijdens het lezen van dit interview. Niet de
gesuggereerde banden met Anne Frank. Ik begrijp dat die gegevens het voor de lezers
duidelijk maakt waar het om gaat.
Maar juist jouw verhaal trof mij. Natuurlijk omdat ik deel van die periode was met mijn
toen zo prille leeftijd van 3 tot 6 jaar.
Maar vooral ook omdat door jouw doorzettingsvermogen jij mij vond in Schagen bij mijn
laatste onderduikouders.
Weet dat ik er zelf heilig van overtuigd ben dat ik me nooit zo had kunnen ontplooien als
jij er niet geweest was.
Dit heb ik jou ook eigenlijk nooit kunnen zeggen. Daar schaam ik me wel voor. Maar ik
hoop dat het nog niet te laat is om dit nu wel te doen.

Zij, de familie Jaspers, gaven mij zo maar aan jou mee. Zij vertrouwde je van meet af
aan. En jij bracht mij terug naar het huis van je ouders, waar mijn moeder toen ook
verbleef.
Stel je voor, een kind dat " zoek was" en andere naam had, moest toch gevonden
worden. En jij deed het. Die namiddag staat mij nog steeds helder voor ogen.
Gelukkig heb ik, tot op de dag van vandaag, het contact met hen en hun kinderen altijd in
stand kunnen houden.

Nog niet zo lang geleden hoorde ik ook over het wel en wee van Loutje. Pas na het
interview begreep ik jouw rol hierin.
O wat was jij flink in die dagen en zo bewust van het pad dat je koos.
En wat jij over je moeder schreef, mijn tante Jo, dat wist ik ook nooit.
Wel weet ik dat een kind van de zuster van je moeder, Jan Arie de Groot , ook diep in het
verzets werk heeft gezeten. Hij noemde zich toen Jack.
Hij woont al heel lang in Spanje en leeft nog. Toen hij een aantal jaren geleden in
Amsterdam was heb ik hem opgezocht.
Nam op advies van vrienden van hem een boterkoek mee (zelf gebakken) in een
trommel die je vader ooit gaf aan het personeel met Sinterklaas.
Dat was een emotionele middag en ook heel goed.

Lieve Carla, wat is het goed dat je nu toch met jouw verhaal naar buiten bent gekomen.
Als iemand zich kan indenken dat er een punt gezet moet worden achter het verleden en
dat je daar niet meer over spreekt, ben ik het.
Maar juist daarom ben ik zo blij dat je het toch hebt gedaan.
Nu maar hopen dat deze moedige stap je niet echt zal opbreken en dat je kinderen en
kleinkinderen je daarbij kunnen opvangen.
Dat het je ook een gevoel van voldoening geeft het toch één maal te hebben gezegd.

Dank je nogmaals en wie weet kan dit lijntje al is het op een laag pitje open blijven,
dat zou ik heel plezierig vinden.

Liefs,

Letter from Wilma, February 2015

The Resistance

The Dutch resistance workers called themselves the underground. The underground was not a structured organization but it consisted of many small loose groups of individuals from all walks of life throughout the country. Most groups were nonviolent, and were comprised of only five or six individuals. It is believed that approximately 100,000 Dutch citizens involved themselves in the underground, but no one really knows for sure.

I was involved in two groups, one coordinated by my cousin Jack de Groot in Rotterdam and one in Amsterdam. It was thanks to Jack that I was able to get help when needed.

Jack de Groot (second from right)

Bounty Hunters

Eight to nine thousand Dutch Jews were betrayed by a group of Dutch nazi sympathizers who were recruited by the Dutch nazi government and organized as bounty hunters. The group of close to 80 members was given a weekly stipend by the nazi government, and received additional payment for each Jew they betrayed. They were all middle-aged men, nicely dressed and well spoken, giving the impression of being trustworthy.

The book pictured above tells of the horrible things the bounty hunters did to their fellow countrymen, who were Jewish, all for the love of money.

Nurse's ID

I studied medical technology at a private college during the war. I had an internship in one of the hospital laboratories in Amsterdam. I realized how important it might be to have a German nurse's uniform and I was able to purchase one at the hospital. I stole a blank German medical registration card and filled it out. The uniform came in very handy: I would wear it when I expected a situation might become dangerous.

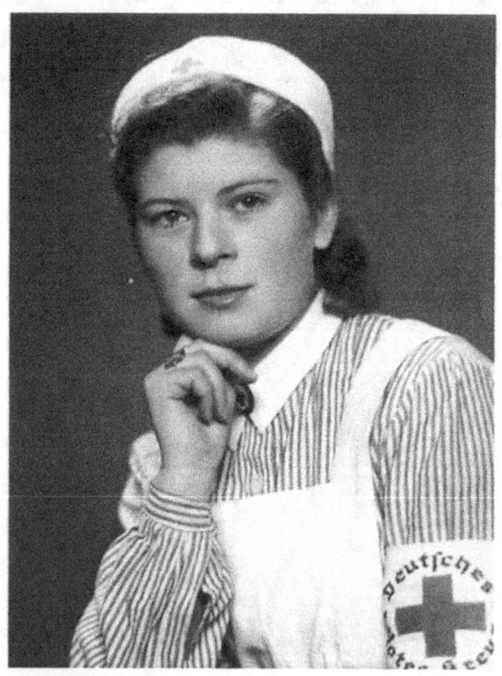

My forged Nurse's Identification in 1944.

An example of a German nurse in uniform

My Cousin Loetje

I vividly remember putting on my nurse's uniform when my Aunt Alie's neighbor notified me that my aunt, one of my father's sisters, and her five children would be stopping on a train at the railway station in Amsterdam.

They had been picked up and were being transported to Westerbork, the transfer camp for Jewish victims. I met the train and was able to locate them. I offered to take the youngest child with me and my aunt gratefully agreed. His name was Loetje Joel and he was 2 1/2 years old.

On the way out of the train station I was stopped by several nazi soldiers and was questioned. I told them Loetje was my son, he was ill, and I was taking him to the hospital. The soldiers accepted my story and let me go.

It was too dangerous for my parents to keep him, so we found him a home. Sadly, Loetje was moved from home to home, many times, during the occupation and consequently did not receive the love and care he needed as a young child.

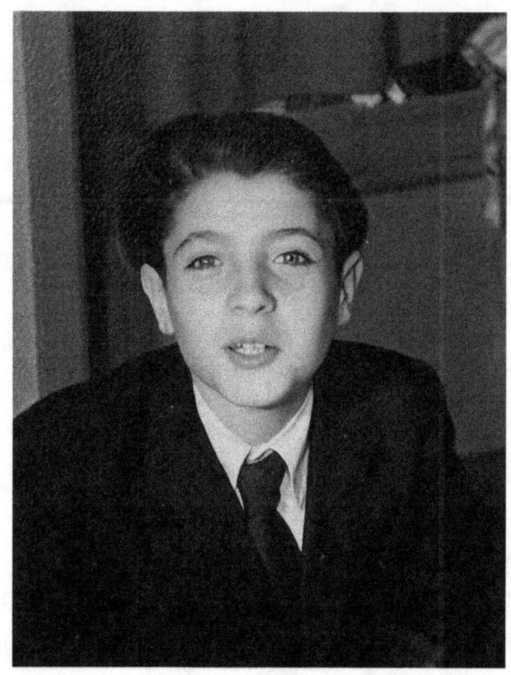

Loetje in 1948

Immediately after the war Loetje became part of our family. My parents were not able to officially adopt him because the Government of the Netherlands took responsibility and oversight for all the war orphans, making them wards of the state. My parents raised him as their own child, and took care of him the rest of his life. Because of the lack of love and care he received during the war; it was very difficult for Loetje to adjust to normal life. He lied, he cheated, he stole, and he had difficulties in school. He became an artist, married, and had one child. Eventually he took his own life.

Forging ID Cards

When people went into hiding, it was critical that they had an ID without a "J" on it. The underground provided me with new ID cards, a small machine to make thumbprints, the seals required on the ID and whatever else was needed. The new ID cards either came from England, dropped by small airplane in the middle of night, or they were stolen. The Queen of the Netherlands, some of the Dutch Cabinet members, her family and staff had fled to England during the German invasion. They were instrumental in the making of and providing these fraudulent ID cards to us in the underground. Not only that, but they also supplied guns, ammunition and anything else the resistance needed.

I became very proficient in creating these forged IDs which were identical in appearance to the official nazi- issued cards. I fabricated approximately 100 of them.

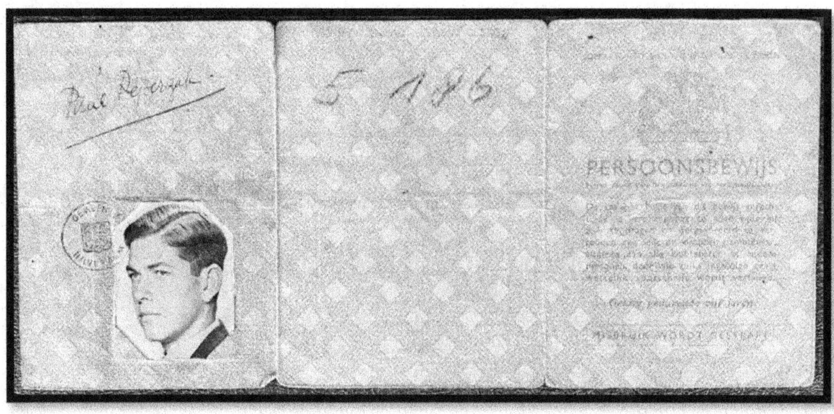

*My husband Paul's official nazi-issued ID card,
September 14, 1941, front and back.*

Dutch Newspapers, Radios, and Cameras

Dutch newspapers were still being printed; however, all the news was from the nazi perspective. The papers were full of propaganda: antisemitic propaganda and exaggerated claims of how well the war was going for the Germans.

The country was flooded daily with nazi falsehoods.

The Dutch people found a great and necessary use for these newspapers. They cut them up and used them for toilet paper since no toilet paper was available in the country.

nazi propaganda in two different newspapers.

1940s Radio

Initially all radios belonging to Jewish people were made illegal and confiscated. Eventually it was illegal for anyone in the Netherlands to have a radio. However some were not turned in. The underground did have some radios. One had to go into a closet to listen to any radio broadcast so that it couldn't be heard. The important broadcast for the underground to listen to was in Dutch from Radio London daily at 6:00 pm. A code would be used to announce to resistance workers when and where a drop of supplies would take place by airplane.

1940s Box Camera

Many of the pictures in this book I took myself. The average citizen was not allowed to use a camera to document life during the War. I chose to take the risk. I was fortunate to be able to have the film developed by a family business I trusted.

Resistance Pamphlets

The underground felt it was very important to inform the public of news and information from the Allies. We were able to get that news from Radio London on the radios we had kept from being confiscated. We took the news and wrote the important points down on a flyer. I was one of the persons who made mimeograph copies for the underground to hand out. Mimeographing copies was a messy process that used a lot of ink, which was sometimes hard to get. Passing out the copies was a very dangerous task.

The underground also created and distributed flyers to counteract some of the the nazi propaganda. The flyer depicted on the facing page is directed at young women asking them to not help the German war effort.

Aan alle meisjes, die de school gaan verlaten

Velen van jullie zullen plannen gemaakt hebben voor de toekomst in verband met je aanleg, verlangen en huiselijke omstandigheden. In deze byzondere tijd zal men zich bij de keuze van een werkkring van nog andere dingen rekenschap moeten geven . . . . . .

1. In vele fabrieken, bedrijven en kantoren wordt uitsluitend (of voor 95 procent) gewerkt voor de bezettende overheid. Zo b.v. in de conservenfabrieken. Ook alle grotere naaiateliers maken kleding voor het duitse volk, terwijl onze huismoeders niet weten, hoe zij hun kinderen moeten kleden.

Alle hulp, die wij geven ten behoeve van het Duitsche Rijk verlengt de oorlog en verarmt ons land.

2. Onze mannen, zoons en broers zijn tewerkgesteld in Duitsland. Op enkele gelukkige uitzonderingen na, hebben zij 't er slecht: lange arbeidsdagen, slechte voeding, onvoldoende verdiensten en zware straffen voor kleine vergrijpen. Velen zullen helaas niet terugkeren.
    Zullen jullie het nu mogelijk maken, dat nog meer van onze mannen weg moeten in een tijd, dat zij zo hard nodig zullen zijn in eigen land?

Weiger elke betrekking aan te nemen, welke in de regel door een mannelijke kracht werd vervuld.

(Op postkantoren en bureaux, als conductrice, brievenbestelster enz.)

3. In verschillende plaatsen worden reeds meisjes opgeroepen om hun gegevens te laten noteren op het arbeidsbureau, zodat zij vandaag of morgen tewerkgesteld kunnen worden in ons land of elders. Dit gebeurde reeds in Zutphen, Arnhem en Nijmegen. In Utrecht werden zij hiervoor onlangs op straat aangehouden.

Zorg er dus voor, dat je niet geregistreerd wordt.

Ook niet, indien je meent veilig te zijn door je baan . . . . . ; dat dachten de mannen ook!

Bovendien moet alle administratie hiervan vertraagd worden.

Er moet echter wél gewerkt worden!

1. In vele huisgezinnen moeten de moeders naast de steun van hun mannen óók nog een goede hulp ontberen.

Help haar zo goed mogelijk door deze tijden heen te komen.

Een vaderlandse daad!

Thuis helpen, zelfs als moeder geen hulp heeft, geeft geen voldoende waarborg voor je veiligheid. **Ruil met een vriendin.**

2. Er is veel werk te verrichten **buiten het Arbeidsbureau om.** Zoek zelf,
    Maar verricht alleen werk ten behoeve van het Nederlandse Volk.

3. Indien mogelijk, volg dan een cursus of opleiding: costuumnaaien, handenarbeid, onderwijzeres, kinderverzorgster, landbouwhuishoudkundige enz. **Je blijft dan scholier.**

Sla deze raadgevingen niet uit **vrees, geldelijk belang, zorgeloosheid of ijdelheid** in de wind. Je dient er de Nederlandse zaak mee.

En dan nog:

Zwijg over alles, wat een ander niet aangaat.

Door babbelzucht zijn reeds heel veel personen, die werken voor de belangen van het Nederlandse volk, vele vervolgden en vele onderduikers in handen van de vijand gevallen . . . . .

Restance Pamphlet for Young Girls
"Do Not Help The German War Effort!"

A 1940s era mimeograph machine.

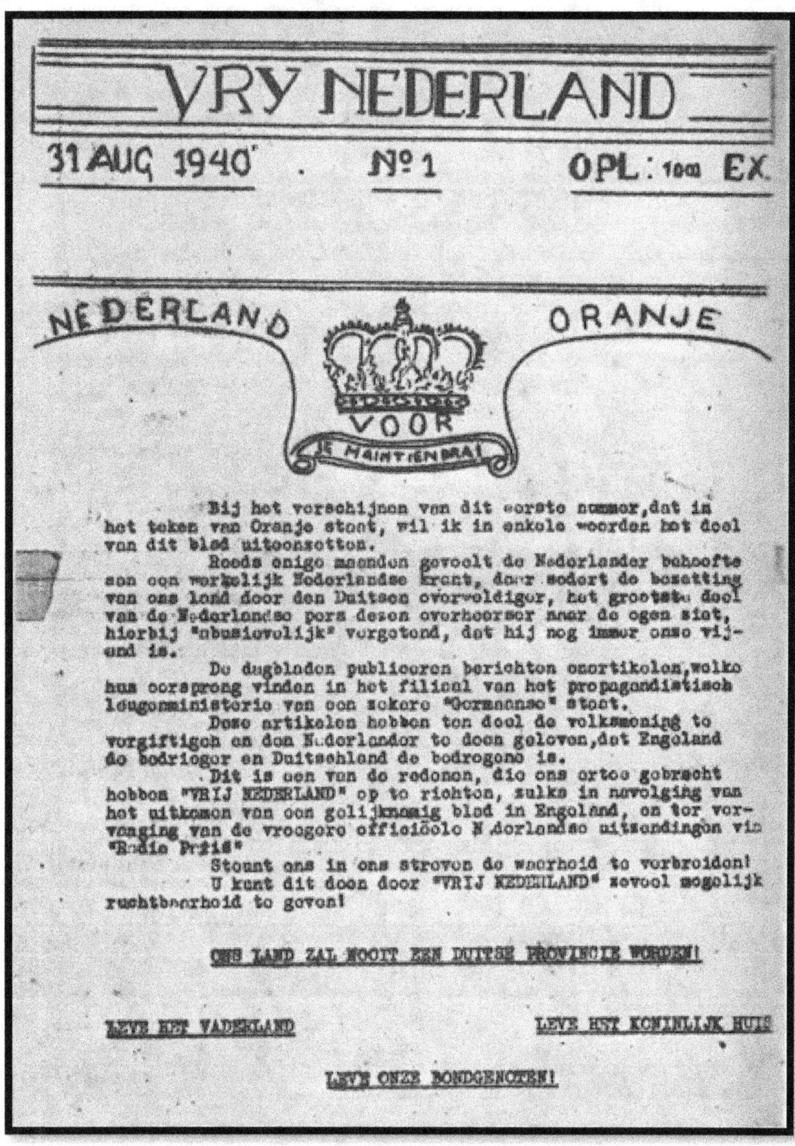

Mimeographed in 1940, this is the first page of the first copy of "Free Netherlands." This periodical is still in print today.

Ration Cards

Food in the Netherlands became harder and harder to get so the only way to buy food was with government-issued ration cards. The people in hiding obviously did not receive any ration cards and the host families could not feed them just on their own. Again, thanks to the resistance movement regularly raiding distribution centers and stealing ration cards, I was able to hand them out to the people I helped in hiding. I usually visited those people once a month, delivering medications, running errands, and bringing them whatever else they might need.

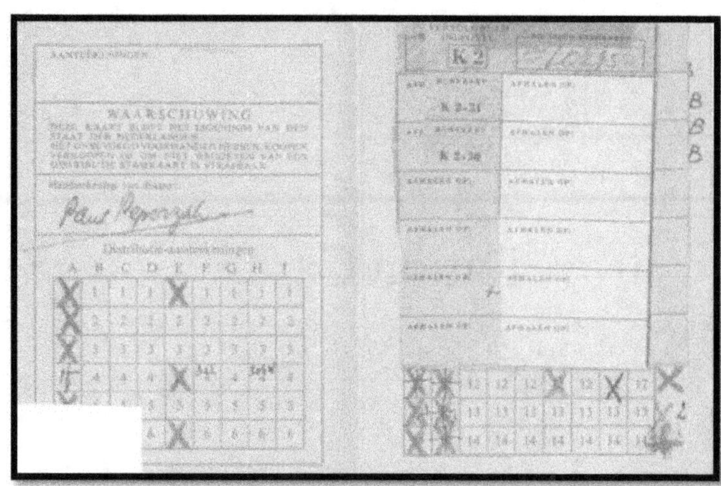

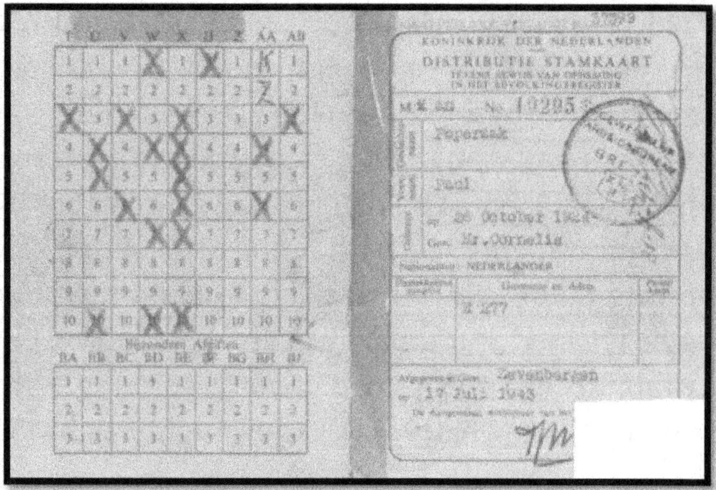

My husband Paul Peperzak's 1943 rations card (front and back) Ration cards were required in order to receive food. One could not eat without a ration card.

In March 1943 the nazi government found out there were about 25,000 Jews in hiding in the Netherlands. They then introduced a "second distribution food card" in January 1944. It was linked to the Dutch ID cards in order to track and prevent Jews in hiding and members of the resistance from getting food.

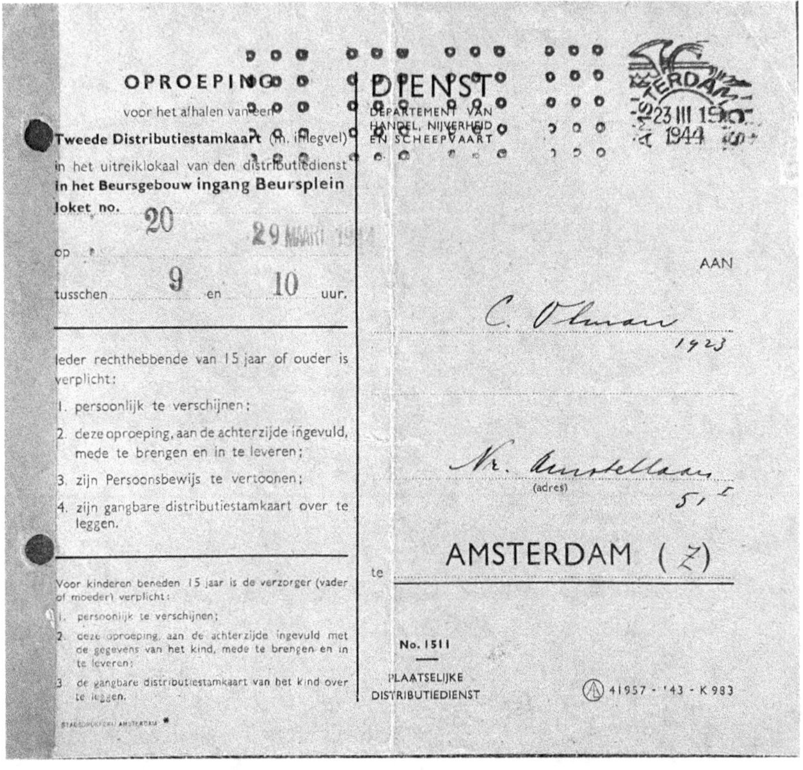

Form To Get Second Food Distribution 1944 (front)

ONTVANGSTBEWIJS

NIET VOUWEN

Ondergeteekende verklaart te hebben ontvangen een Tweede Distributiestamkaart (met inlegvel) ten name van:

1. Geslachtsnaam

2. Voornamen

3. Geboren op _______ dag _______ maand _______ jaar , te _______

4. Ongehuwd, gehuwd, gescheiden, weduwstaat (doorhalen wat niet van toepassing is)

5. Aantal inwonende kinderen beneden 15 jaar: _______ jongens, _______ meisjes

6. Woonplaats **Amsterdam**

7. Provincie **Noord-Holland**

8. Straat en huisnummer:

9. Beroep

10. Werkgever (Firma)

te

INVULLEN MET BLOKLETTERS

11. No. Persoonsbewijs

12. No. gangbare distr. stamk.

13. Niet invullen

Datum: _______ Handteekening: _______

(datum en handteekening eerst bij het afhalen van de distributiestamkaart invullen)

Form to get second food distribution (back)

1000 & 500 Guilder Note

Things didn't always go smoothly for me with the people I helped hide. Those in hiding had to have money to help support themselves. It was easier to carry and hide large denomination notes than small ones. Towards the latter part of the war the nazis decided to withdraw the large denomination notes and gave people 3 months to exchange those notes into smaller denominations. Several of my people in hiding asked me to do the exchanges for them.

One man in particular gave me a total of 20,000 guilders to change. That would be $348,000 in today's money (2024). Because of my young age I was not able to go to a bank with that large amount of money so I asked the resistance to help me. I received back only 50% of the original value of the money to give to him. When the war was over, an attorney for the man I did the exchange for demanded the balance of his 20,000 guilders. My father and I went to the attorney and explained that I had not kept a penny, and had been grateful to get 50% of the amount I had been entrusted with. The attorney realized there was no case, and no follow up occurred. The money was another casualty of the war.

Paul Peperzak, My Husband

I did not meet my husband Paul Peperzak until after the war. He was not Jewish. Paul was studying tropical agriculture when the universities were all closed during the war.

Paul Peperzak

In April of 1943 the Dutch nazi Government required all Dutch university students to sign a loyalty declaration to the nazi government: eighty five percent of the students refused to do so. As a result all public universities were closed. The male students along with most of the young men in the country were forced to go to work camps in Germany to work for the German war effort. The workers were treated as slaves. It was rare to see a young man on the streets after that.

University of Wageningen

University students at Wageningen. My husband Paul is the first man on the left.

Because Paul was studying agriculture he went to work for a farmer. The Germans gave him permission to work on the farm because farm workers were needed. Sadly, most of the Dutch farm products were confiscated and sent to Germany, leaving only a little for the Dutch population.

One of Paul's tasks on the farm was milking cows. He hated that job the most because he was afraid of being kicked by a cow.

Even though he had the exemption he was still arrested twice and taken into custody to be questioned. The first time he was arrested, Paul chewed some tobacco which gave him an asthma attack. The Germans then let him go, giving him a medical exemption.

Paul milking a cow

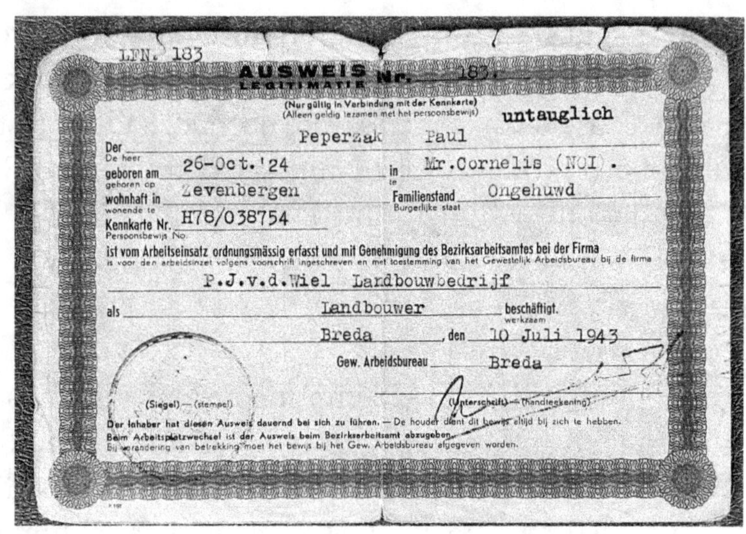

Paul's Exemption Pass (Ausweis)

The second time Paul was arrested he was being inter-
viewed by a nazi officer who was briefly called away from
the interrogation room. A sympathetic German soldier
showed Paul a back door and told him to run. Paul spent
the rest of the war in hiding, which he did in his parents'
home.

Leni Van Kleef

My friend Leni van Kleef

One of my friends, Leni van Kleef, lived in Den Haag (The Hague) with her husband and young son. Her husband had already been seized and deported to one of the concentration camps. Leni was pregnant and went to a small private clinic to deliver her baby. While at the clinic, shortly after giving birth, two SS officers went to her house to pick her up. The neighbors were forced to tell the officers which clinic she was at, and they then called the clinic to warn her. Leni got up, dressed and left the clinic without her 24 hour old newborn. She passed the officers in the street without them recognizing who she was. When the officers realized she was not at the clinic they took the infant girl to Westerbork.

I received a desperate call from Leni asking if I could retrieve the baby from nazi hands. My uncle, who was detained in Westerbork working in the hospital there, sent a message to me through the underground to warn me of the danger if I continued to try to rescue the baby.

Two weeks after the birth Leni gave herself up along with her little boy, and was reunited with the baby in Westerbork. From Westerbork they were sent on to one of concentration camps. Amazingly all three survived and returned to the Netherlands after the war. Unfortunately, Leni had cancer and passed away a couple of months after her return.

Anne Frank

Anne Frank and her family lived around the corner from where I lived with my family prior to the Frank family going into hiding. Anne was five years younger than me; her sister Margot was much closer to me in age. I met and got to know them through our Reform Synagogue in Amsterdam. Margot and I were in the same religion classes at temple. Sometimes our Hebrew lessons were at our Rabbi Mehler's home. I did get to know Anne during rehearsals and performances of several plays that were held by the Temple.

Margot was also a rower, though she was not a member of Poseidon. Margot and I enjoyed each other's company. I was invited to their home several times. I distinctly remember noticing their heavy furniture from their large home in Germany did not fit well in the smaller Dutch apartment.

The photos shown here are the way I remember Margot and Anne.

Margot Frank (Anne's older sister) sunbathing on their apartment roof before the war.

Anne Frank on the roof top. This is the way I remember her. She is the author of the most-read diary and account of the Holocaust.

SS Interrogation

I was always afraid. I was stopped several times for various reasons. I particularly remember one very scary situation. Two nazi officers came to interrogate me about my activities. They asked many questions which I answered in such a way as not to implicate me. I spoke fluent German at the time, and I have never been a flirt, but I flirted with them as they interrogated me. They must have been taken in by my flirtations because they became friendly and gallant. I managed to convince them I was innocent. I needed to leave when they did. I was carrying my briefcase which held the supplies I used to make forged ID cards. One of the officers gallantly offered to carry my briefcase for me and I had no choice but to let him do it. Fortunately, the officers never looked inside the case, and it did not fall open. Had it opened I would not be here writing this today.

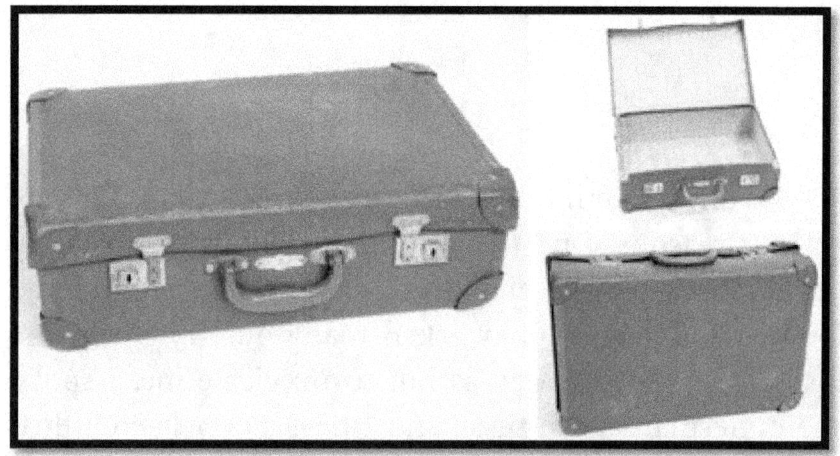

1940s Suitcase.

Courier Work

An example of matched paper.

Occasionally I was asked to do courier work. This required me to carry papers and other important secret documents to another out-of-town member of the resistance. One way to confirm we were passing these items to the correct person was by the use of a piece of paper that had been cut in a unique way: the cut edge on my piece of paper had to match the cut edge of the recipient's piece.

Surnames were never used in order to prevent a member of the resistance from identifying other members in case they were caught. Often first names were changed.

A statue honoring the girls and women who did the dangerous courier work in WWII, located in Leeuwarden, Netherlands.

Most of the work I did was by bicycle because it was the safest mode of transportation. If I was on my bicycle and saw something suspicious or dangerous I could change direction immediately. Eventually the tires wore out and

I needed new ones: they were almost impossible to find or buy. However I was lucky. One of the resistance groups raided a beet sugar factory not far from Amsterdam and they gave me some of the stolen sugar. I distributed it to the people in hiding that I was helping. I was able to keep some for myself. I used the sugar to barter for some new bicycle tires.

An identical representation of my 1940s bicycle.

Bartering

Bartering began when the food supply became sparse. Most of the food was being taken and sent to Germany. My sister Miep regularly went on her bike to farmers to barter for milk and eggs in exchange for linens, clothing, and many other items. She met her future husband Dave Philips on one of these trips.

A Dutch farm in the 1940s.

Pearl Harbor

I was always afraid, but I was always full of hope that the nazis would lose the war. The nazi regime was so brutal and destructive that I refused to believe they could prevail.

Everyone in Western Europe was incredibly grateful that the Japanese attacked Pearl Harbor because the Americans then declared war on Germany and joined the Allied forces. We knew then that Germany could not possibly win.

JAPANESE BOMB PEARL HARBOR!

Hickam, Wheeler, Kaneohe Hit

The USS Arizona, burning after her forward magazines exploded, sank with nearly 1,200 hands lost.

'When I Came to, the Ship Was a Mass of Flames...'

Eyewitness Accounts of Brutal Bombing From Around Oahu

Officers were eating breakfast aboard the USS Arizona when a short signal on the ship's air raid alarm sounded.

"As I was running forward on the starboard side of the quarterdeck... I was apparently knocked out by the blast of a bomb," said Lt. Cmdr. G. Fuqua, the senior surviving officer.

The bomb was one of eight that hit the 26-year-old battleship.

"When I came to, and got up off the deck, the ship was a mass of flames amidships on the boat deck," he said.

Fuqua said he tried to extinguish flames in the gun turrets, but found the water main had no water. Seventy wounded men were taken from the ruptured decks and sent to hospitals before Fuqua ordered all hands to abandon ship at 9 a.m.

Horrendous Injuries

Wounded victims poured into the Army's Tripler General Hospital. Corridors were soon jammed with the wounded and dying, many left on the floor.

The injuries came from shrapnel wounds suffered as bombs fell, direct hits from machine-gun strafing by enemy planes, and our own anti-aircraft fire. Chunks of metal were lodged in necks, in chests, through legs.

Because of a severe shortage of gauze, bandage, morphine and other medical supplies like amputating saws, surgeons made do with what they could for the first part of the day. They lifted stretchers themselves when orderlies weren't available, held victims down together on the way to surgery when there were no splints and, in one instance, held open a vessel being catheterized with a finger.

Abandon ship

Aboard the USS Utah, the

Blood Donors Are Urgently Needed

An urgent call for blood to be used in transfusions has been made by Queen's Hospital.

Any person willing to donate blood is asked to make his way to the hospital and go to the fourth floor.

flag was being raised as the first planes were spotted.

"Immediately thereafter, the

Fire all too real

France Ordonnez was playing football outside his family's
(See Back Page, Col. 1)

MORE THAN 2,000 DIE IN SNEAK AIR ATTACK

Scores of low-flying Japanese planes swooped down on Oahu from the north 90 minutes after dawn today in a surprise attack, raining bombs and terror on Pearl Harbor and other military installations.

Before it was over, the huge U.S. Pacific Fleet lay crippled at anchor and nearby air fields were heavily damaged.

The raid by planes with the Rising Sun emblem of Japan clearly visible on their wingtips left more than 2,000 American soldiers, sailors and Marines dead or missing and more than 1,000 grievously injured.

The attackers poured their fury of bombs and torpedoes primarily on military facilities.

In Honolulu, bomb or artillery fragments rained down on civilian populations, leveling two housing areas more than two miles apart, and blowing up bits of homes far from the military bases. A bomb or errant shell fell near Iolani Palace, creating a crater on the Palace grounds.

Dozens of civilians are believed dead due to enemy action, explosions, fires and mishaps in the wake of the attack.

President Roosevelt announced the attack to the nation, and is expected to ask for a declaration of war on Japan tomorrow in an address to a joint session of Congress. Early today, the Territory of Hawaii was put under martial law.

Tonight, a torn, blacked-out Hawaii braced for further attack or even an invasion of the islands. The whereabouts of the Japanese fleet that is believed to have launched this morning's raid remain unknown, officials said.

Battleships ravaged

The Japanese warplanes spent their greatest fury on the big ships berthed around Ford Island.

A huge armor-piercing bomb blew up the USS Arizona, enveloping its bow in chilling flames. The battleship sank in less than nine minutes, entombing nearly 1,000 sailors and Marines in a watery grave. Another 300 were lost on deck.

Torpedoes ripped through the USS Oklahoma, rolling her over and imprisoning more men within.

The battleships California and West Virginia, wrapped in flames, sank at their moorings. The target ship Utah capsized with many of its crewmen still aboard.

Harbor horror chamber

Within minutes, the fiery, oil-laden harbor was turned into a watery horror chamber of broken and burned bodies.

Men in varying states of shock and injury jumped from their ships and swam to boats or nearby shores to cheat death.

Navy boat crews searched the waters around the burning ships and made countless trips
(See Back Page, Col.1)

Martial Law Is Declared for Territory

Civilians Arrested

Faced with the prospect of invasion and sabotage, Gen. Joseph B. Poindexter today declared the Territory of Hawaii to be under martial law.

Censorship is in place, a blackout and curfew have been imposed and all citizens are commanded to obey orders of military officials.

Some suspected enemy agents or sympathizers have already been arrested and detained under martial law rules. Lt. Gen. Walter C. Short, commanding general of the Hawaiian Department, urged Poindexter to declare the state of emergency during a meeting in the governor's office at Iolani Palace shortly after noon.

The governor, after a radio telephone consultation with President Roosevelt, agreed. Short briefed military government
(See Back Page, Col. 6)

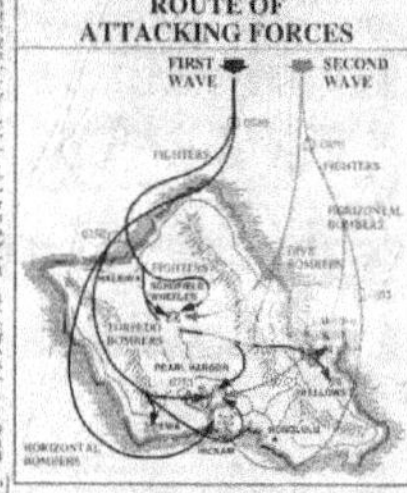

Japan declares a state of war

United Press reported that Tokyo radio has declared that a state of war exists between Japan and British and United States Powers in the Pacific. Japanese forces also attacked in Malaya, the Philippines, Hong Kong, Midway, Wake, and Guam, according to news service reports.

Five U.S. Navy planes shot down

HONOLULU — Anti-aircraft batteries opened fire on a squadron of six U.S. Navy planes approaching Ford Island just before 9 p.m., shooting down five of them. At least three of the six Navy pilots are dead. The planes, launched off the carrier USS Enterprise, were landing after searching in vain for the Japanese fleet.

Stimson orders Army into uniform

WASHINGTON — Secretary of War Henry L. Stimson tonight ordered the entire U.S. Army into uniform — 1,600,000 men, including thousands of officers and men on duty in administrative posts who have been allowed civilian clothes.

Food Drops

In June of 1944 the Allied Forces invaded Normandy. In September of that year they arrived in the Netherlands and liberated the southern part of the country. They were not able to cross the rivers to northern Netherlands because of the fierce fighting of the Germans. It took another eight months to liberate the northern part of the country which included the three biggest cities of Amsterdam, Rotterdam and The Hague.

American Plane "Air Drop" of Food, 1945

That winter prior to final liberation was horrible. There was no food left other than sugar beets. The beets needed to be cooked for hours to become edible. There was no fuel, no gas, and no electricity. The winter of 1944/45 was one of the coldest winters on record. All the trees in the cities and country were cut down to burn for heat, along with wood from empty homes, furniture, charcoal found between railroad tracks etc. The North Sea froze over. Approximately 25,000 people starved to death. It was known as the Hunger Winter.

During the last ten days of the war prior to the German surrender the Allied forces received permission to airdrop 11,000 tons of food into the still occupied northern part of the Netherlands to help alleviate the famine. It took several years following the war to cure the hunger that the Dutch had suffered.

Prisoner Of War Camp

At the end of the war, the Dutch government confined Dutch nazis and collaborators in a prisoner of war camp that had been previously used as a prison camp by the Germans in the town of Amersfoort.

The Dutch government hired me to be the only medical officer of the camp. By then I was a licensed medical technologist.

What little food was available after the war was atrocious. I received many requests from the prisoners for special diets, hoping the food would be better. I took sweet revenge on the prisoners by requiring them to have their stomachs pumped without anesthesia, not just once but two times to determine if there was a real need for a special diet. Pretty soon the requests stopped.

I worked in the camp for several months before joining the Blood Transfusion Service, a division of the Nurse's Corps of the Royal Dutch Army. My work there included visiting the military bases throughout the Netherlands to draw blood and do blood typing on all the new recruits. We also did research on the Rh factor.

I worked on staff in Amersfoort as a medical officer.

On one occasion while working at a military base one of the young officers fainted as I drew his blood. At lunch, he chose to retaliate for the embarrassment of fainting by offering me my first airplane ride, and we left right away. His revenge included a lot of acrobatics midair which caused me to be very airsick. Upon landing he told me to clean up the mess I had made or pay to have the plane cleaned. I paid. I was happy to never see the man again.

I drew blood for blood typing from newly enlisted soldiers after the war at least twice a week.
This photo was taken Kamp Valkenburg.

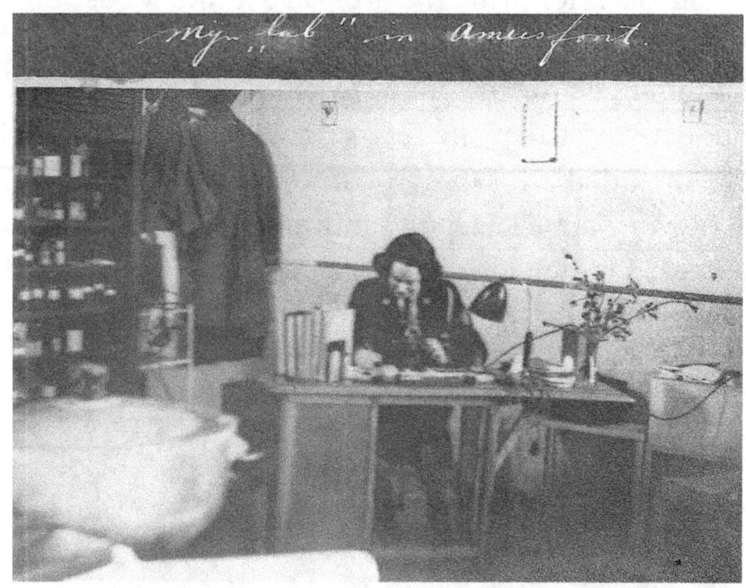

A photo of me working in my lab in Amersfoort.

The detention camp in Amersfoort

Appie

My sister Miep's first husband Dave passed away in his early 50's. My sister then spent the rest of her life with Appie Mof, a relative by marriage. In 1997 Appie walked by a neighborhood bookstore in Amsterdam and, to his shock, he saw a book in the bookstore window called "Joods Amsterdam" (Jewish Amsterdam), published that year, with a photo of his sister's 1937 wedding as the cover. He was understandably very upset. Everything in his parents' home was stolen after his parents, sister and brother-in-law were deported to one of the concentration camps, where they were murdered.

Appie managed to escape the Netherlands, traveling by foot, bicycle, bus, and train to Portugal. He boarded a ship to Cuba where he stayed for some time, then traveled to New York, where he enlisted in the Dutch division of the Canadian Army. He served as an airplane mechanic in England for the rest of the war.

Appie tried unsuccessfully to find out how the cover photo and another family photo in the book ended up in the hands of the book's author. After Appie passed away Miep's grandson Gilbert was able to track down the author's wife, who refused to speak to him. To date we still don't know where the authors found the photos.

My brother-in-law's family wedding photo mysteriously appeared on the cover of "Joods Amsterdam" (Jewish Amsterdam), a book published in 1992. The photo was stolen from their house along with the home's entire contents after the family was deported to the death camps.

My New Life

I met my husband Paul Peperzak in the library at the University of Amsterdam in 1946. I wanted to become a medical doctor and was studying to take the medical school entrance exams. Paul was writing a paper on cocoa. We were married in 1947 just prior to Paul leaving for Ames, Iowa to work on a master's degree in agronomy. He had received a scholarship to go there from the Institute of International Education. Once in Iowa he found a gentleman to sponsor my visitor's visa to the US and I followed Paul four months later.

We moved to Liberia, West Africa after Paul received his master's degree and accepted a job from Firestone Rubber Plantations. The first two of our four children were born in Liberia. The other two were born in Iowa when Paul returned to the States to pursue a PhD.

We became American citizens in Hawaii in 1958. From then on my husband's career in tropical agriculture gave us the opportunity to live in several countries around the world. We retired to Colorado Springs, Colorado in 1987.

November 13, 1958: Naturalization Day for the Peperzak Family in Honolulu, Hawaii.

I moved to Spokane, WA in 2004 to be close to my oldest daughter Marian Cummings after Paul passed away. It was here in Spokane that I realized how important it is to educate people about the Holocaust by telling my story.

My Sweet Revenge

Carla's 100th Birthday Celebration with her family in Colorado Springs, Colorado.

I am often asked what my revenge against nazi Germany would be. Hitler's primary goal was to eliminate all Jews. My revenge is my family: 4 married children, 11 married grandchildren, and 22 great grandchildren!

Respect!

The Oxford Dictionary defines respect as 'due regard for the feelings, wishes, rights or traditions of others'.

My wish is that everyone who reads this book will find it in themselves to respect others. If we all can respect every person, young or old, like or dislike, understand or not understand, different in skin color, religion, or language, agree or disagree, human or creature, the result will be understanding, no hate, no bullying, no wars, no killing, no genocide. If you respect someone you would never consider killing them.

Never again.

A mural depicting me at Carla Olman Peperzak Middle School in Spokane, Washington, created by the 2023/2024 sixth and seventh grade art classes.

My family celebrating my 99th birthday with a visit to the Carla Olman Peperzak Middle School in Spokane, Washington while it was still under construction, November 2022

Holocaust Remembrance

Prompt: "Create an original piece of art influenced by the lifesaving actions of one or more young heroes of the Holocaust."

The young heroes that were recommended and used to inspire the many works of art included Spokane's Car-

la Peperzak and Hannie Schafer, sisters Truus and Freddie Oversteegen, and Sophie Scholl. This prompt was for 2024's annual Yom Hashoa art contest sponsored by Temple Beth Shalom in Spokane.

The artist, Mackenzie Winchel, creator of the leaded glass artwork, won the contest and the piece now hangs in Peperzak Middle School. Mackenzie wrote the following description of her piece.

"My piece was inspired by the brave actions of these girls who at the time of their actions were the same age as me. As I read about the lives they saved and what they did, I had to ask myself if I could be that brave in the same situation.

Carla skated in the canals as a girl, and the Oversteegen sisters and Hannie would have made memories there as well. The water underneath flows and inspires hope, and the currents are as strong as the bravery it took to lure nazis into the woods and hide family in farmhouses. Hidden in the water are roses in honor of Sophie Scholl, a resistance fighter for the White Rose Movement who was brave enough to stand up and distribute anti-nazi information and was beheaded for her actions.

It can be hard to do the right thing, let alone as heroic as standing up to nazis, especially when you are young. The actions of Carla, Hannie, Truus, Freddie and Sophia directly resulted in generations of more young people who both survived and exist because of their actions, and who are inspired to do the right thing looking at their actions.

The rays of color beaming out of the bridge represent those generations. I selected bright, warm, and cool colors to inspire hope. I wanted it to represent the hope heroes, like Carla Peperzak, create, as well as be mindful of the loss that came out of the Holocaust. The title of my piece, 'Ometz,' is a Hebrew word for courage.

Carla Peperzak's actions will inspire generations of students who will be inspired by her story over and over as they walk the halls of the school named for her and her bravery. This is also why I am donating the piece to Peperzak Middle School—as a colorful, hopeful reminder that being brave enough to do the right thing can make anyone a hero, and in honor of Carla's 100th birthday year. Which is something I kept in mind as I designed and chose the bright warm and cool colors—I wanted it to represent the hope heroes create, as well as be mindful of the loss that came out of the Holocaust."

Awards, Degrees, and Letters of Appreciation

Cannes Film Festival Nomination for movie about my life. The award-winning feature documentary, Carla the Rescuer. I am here with Kristine Hoover, co-producer of the documentary "Carla the Rescuer."

The Cannes Film Festival Nominated movie was created and produced by Kristine Hoover, Professor and Chair of Gonzaga University's School of Leadership Studies and Clement Lye, Associate Director of Production and Emerging Media at Gonzaga University.

The link to the movie documenting my story is at https://carlatherescuer.org/

BEVELHEBBER

NEDERLANDSCHE STRIJDKRACHTEN

HOOFDKWARTIER TE VELDE

1945

This letter was sent to me with a medal from Prins Bernard Of The Netherlands, 1945

Hoofdintendance
BT-BS-SG-G10
Hoofdintendant tel. 95528
Afd.: Voorraden en Panden 27892-27100
Afd. Vervoer   Tel. 97800-20085
Afd.: Bakkerijen en Keukens {
Afd.: Inkoop en Vordering   { 20096

Amsterdam, 8 Juni   1945.

VERKLARING.

Mej.C.Olman, Frederikaplein 50 te Amsterdam heeft
zich in de afgelopen jaren onderscheiden in de strijd tegen den
bezetter. Haar medewerking bestond vooral in het onderbrengen en
het verzorgen van ondergedoken joden; het overbrengen van kran-
ten; het klaarmaken van persoonsbewijzen en verdere koeriers-
diensten.

Nu Mej.Olman zich gaarne bij de Marva ingeschakeld
zag, moge ik de betreffende autoriteiten verzoeken, haar de
grootst mogelijke medewerking te willen verlenen.
Persoonlijk sta ik in voor haar idealistische doel-
stelling. Dit was de aanleiding voor haar soms zeer moedig optre-
den tijdens de bezetting ; ongetwijfeld zal dit ook haar richt-
snoer bij de thans door haar gekozen richting zijn.

De Chef Vervoer Hoofdintendance

BT – BS – SG – G.10

Rob Wagenaar

(ROb K.P.)

I.H.V.A. A'dam

*Office of the Underground, Netherlands Royal Dutch Army
Service Corps, 8 June 1945*

DECLARATION

Miss C. Olman, Frederikplein 50 in Amsterdam distinguished herself in during the past years in the fight against the occupier. Her contribution existed especially in finding shelter and taken care of Jews in hiding; delivery of newspapers; preparation of identity cards; and other couriers services.

Miss Olman wishes to join the Marva, I request the authorities give her special assistance.

Personally, I guarantee her idealistic purpose. This was the reason for her very brave and courageous performance during the occupation; without a doubt this will also be her attitude in her choice of the direction she wants to go.

Chief Transportation Head Army Service Corps.
BT-BS-BG-G.10
Rob Wagemaar

English translation of the letter from the Office of the Underground of 8 June, 1945.

WASHINGTON STATE SENATE

SENATE RESOLUTION
8623

By Senators Billig, Baumgartner, Cleveland, Jayapal, Conway, Chase, Hasegawa, Liias, McCoy, Hargrove, Hatfield, Kohl-Welles, Keiser, Mullet, Pedersen, McAuliffe, Fraser, Nelson, Rolfes, Padden, Parlette, Dammeier, Brown, O'Ban, Becker, Fain, Rivers, Schoesler, Sheldon, Hewitt, Hill, Benton, Roach, Warnick, Dansel, Darneille, and Litzow

WHEREAS, When she was only a teenager, Carla Olman Peperzak was a Jewish member of the Dutch Resistance during World War II who saved at least 40 people from Nazi persecution; and

WHEREAS, In 1940, Peperzak was 16 and living in Holland when the Nazi occupation started, the country which had the highest Jewish fatality rate of Western Europe in World War II; and

WHEREAS, Peperzak dedicated herself to protecting others, frequently and fearlessly placing her own life in danger; and

WHEREAS, Equipped with stolen German identification papers and a German nurse's uniform, Peperzak became active in the Resistance, forging identification papers, serving as a messenger for the underground movement, and helping publish a newsletter of Allied Forces' activities, all at perilous risk to her own safety; and

WHEREAS, During the course of her missions, Peperzak was stopped at least three times while in disguise, the first when she rescued her 2-year-old cousin who had been taken by the Nazis, and she escaped by using resourcefulness to distract German officers; and

WHEREAS, Peperzak became a United States citizen in 1958 and moved to Spokane in 2004; and

WHEREAS, Peperzak now speaks publicly and passionately about her experiences at schools in Eastern Washington and Idaho, and shares her story to educate the next generations and because there are few Holocaust survivors remaining;

NOW, THEREFORE, BE IT RESOLVED, That the Washington State Senate honor and recognize Carla Olman Peperzak as a selfless and brave hero, who saved the lives of many and is now using her experiences to speak to new generations and educate us all about our history and the human capacity to care for others while facing unimaginably difficult challenges.

I, Hunter G. Goodman, Secretary of the Senate,
do hereby certify that this is a true and
correct copy of Senate Resolution 8623,
adopted by the Senate
March 10, 2015

HUNTER G. GOODMAN
Secretary of the Senate

Washington State Senate Resolution 8623, March 2015

JAY INSLEE
Governor

STATE OF WASHINGTON
Office of the Governor

Greetings from the Governor
February 20th, 2020

I am pleased to extend warm greetings to all of those attending the 2020 Association of Washington Generals Award Reception. I am supremely excited about the award recipients for this year.

I count it a privilege to have such vibrant and diverse organizations and individuals in the state of Washington, and I am thankful for the part that each of you plays in establishing a rich community in our state. The contributions that each of you make to our community are truly some of Washington's greatest strengths.

I would especially like to recognize Carla Peperzak, who will receive the Washingtonian of the Year Award. Carla is a survivor of the Holocaust and was a member of the Dutch Resistance in WWII, taking part in the courageous fight against Nazi-occupied Holland. She became a citizen of the United States in 1958 and moved to Spokane in 2004. She has been a frequent public speaker, educating communities throughout the state about the perils of the Holocaust. At 96 years old, she is one of the few remaining Holocaust survivors in the world.

I would also like to specifically recognize Hilltop Artists for being recognized as the 2020 Organization of the Year. They are a non-profit glass arts program that provides classes for over 650 students each year. The tuition-free program combines artistic instruction in glass-blowing with community outreach and support services, with a special emphasis on serving individuals experiencing homelessness, substance abuse disorders, and physical abuse or neglect.

Finally, I would like to recognize Former Mayor Doreen Marchione. Her contributions, as CEO of Hopelink, within Redmond and Kirkland city governments, as well as her many other positions, will forever be etched into the history of Washington State.

Thank you once again for attending today's reception, and may the year ahead bring you good health, peace, and continued service.

Very truly yours,

Jay Inslee
Governor

Washingtonian of the Year January 2020

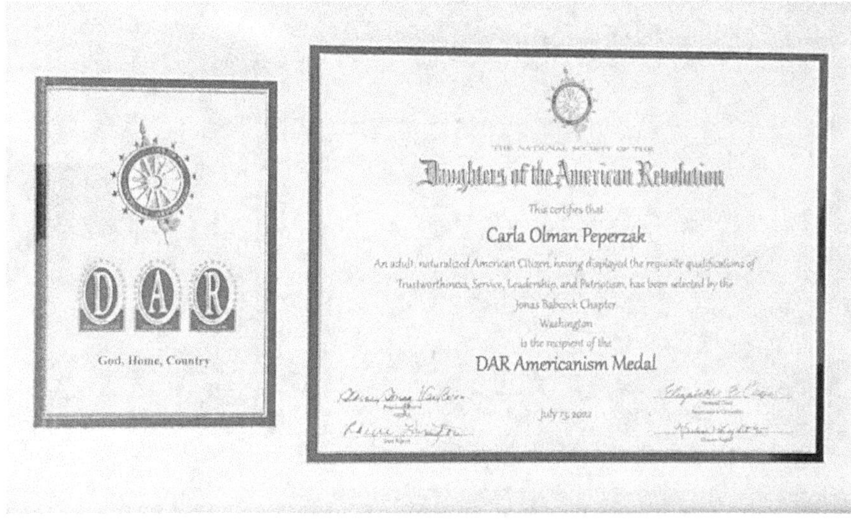

Daughters of the American Revolution (DAR) presented me the "Americanism Medal" in July 2022.

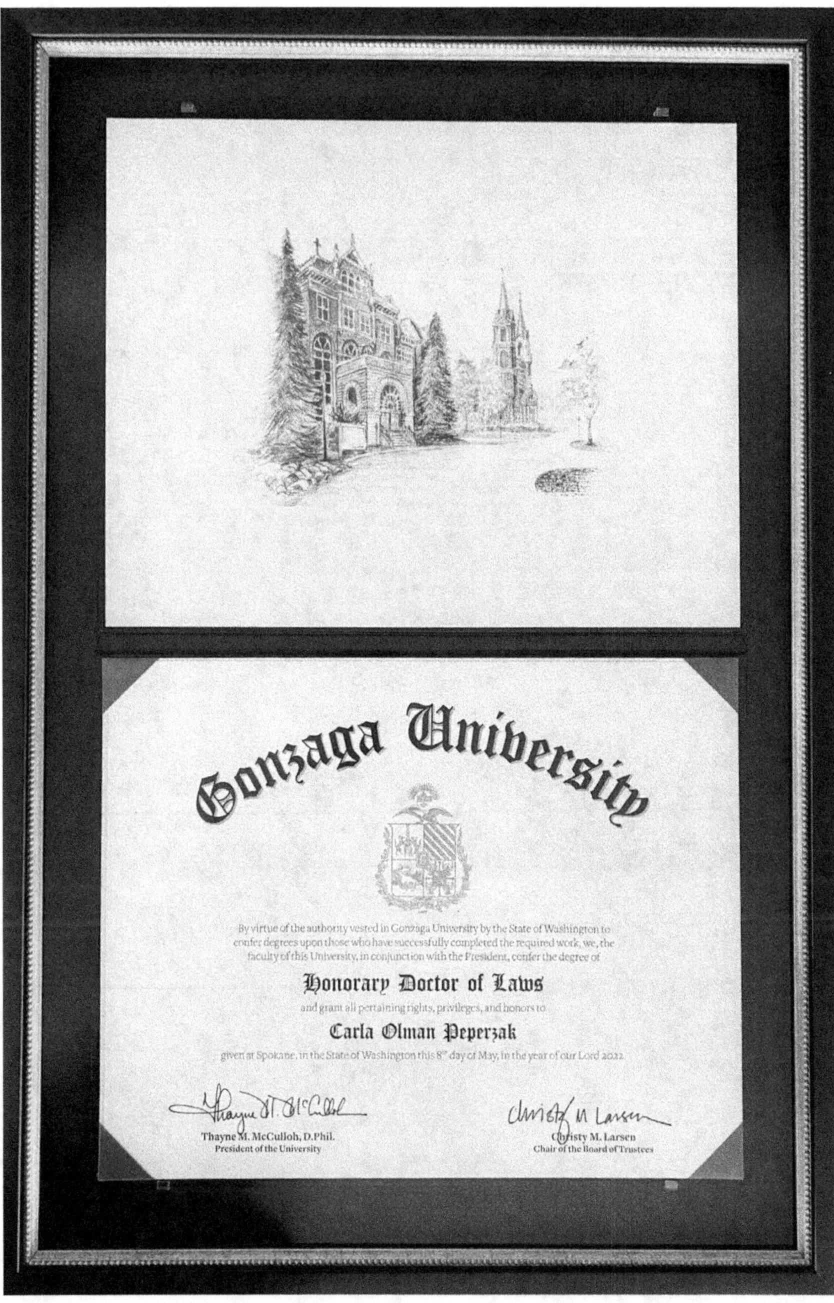

Honorary Doctorate, Gonzaga University, May 2022.

*Honorary Doctorate, Washington State University,
May 2024.*

Permissions and References

- Photos from the archives, with permission from NIOD Institut Voortrekker Oorlogs-Holocaust-en-Genocide Studies, Amsterdam, NIOD.nl

- Photo of Westerbork Camp, courtesy of Holocaust Encyclopedia, United States Holocaust Memorial Museum. Photos of Westerbork Camp, courtesy of Holocaust Encyclopedia, United States Holocaust Museum

- Photo #20190227 "Koerierster door Tineke Bot Leeuwarden.jpg", courtesy of Wikimedia. Photo #20190227 "Koerierster door Tineke Bot Leeuwarden, courtesy of Wikimedia.

- "Shedding Our Stars: The Story of Hans Calmeyer and How He Saved Thousands of Families Like Mine" by Laureen Nussbaum.

- "Boys in the Boat" by Daniel James Brown.

- "De Bezetting" by Dr. L. De Jong. Photos with permission from NIOD Instituut Voortrekker Oorlogs Holocaust en Genocide Studies, Amsterdam, NIOD.nl.

- Photo of the leaded glass art piece, with permission from the artist Mackenzie Winchell.
- Photos of Anne and Margot Frank, with permission from @ANNEFRANKFONDS, Basel, Switzerland.